SERUM WHICH INSTIGATES TOTAL CELLULAR HIJACK

Other books in the S.W.I.T.C.H. series:

Spider Stampede

Grasshopper Glitch

Ant Attack

Crane Fly Crash

Beetle Blast

S.W.I.T.C.H.
SERUM WHICH INSTIGATES TOTAL CELLULAR HIJACK

Fly Frenzy

Ali Sparkes

illustrated by
Ross Collins

OXFORD
UNIVERSITY PRESS

OXFORD
UNIVERSITY PRESS

Great Clarendon Street, Oxford OX2 6DP
Oxford University Press is a department of the University of Oxford.
It furthers the University's objective of excellence in research, scholarship,
and education by publishing worldwide in

Oxford   New York

Auckland   Cape Town   Dar es Salaam   Hong Kong   Karachi
Kuala Lumpur   Madrid   Melbourne   Mexico City   Nairobi
New Delhi   Shanghai   Taipei   Toronto

With offices in

Argentina   Austria   Brazil   Chile   Czech Republic   France   Greece
Guatemala   Hungary   Italy   Japan   Poland   Portugal   Singapore
South Korea   Switzerland   Thailand   Turkey   Ukraine   Vietnam

Oxford is a registered trade mark of Oxford University Press
in the UK and in certain other countries

Text © Ali Sparkes 2011
Illustrations © Ross Collins
S.W.I.T.C.H. logo designed by Dynamo Ltd

The moral rights of the author have been asserted

Database right Oxford University Press (maker)

First published 2011

British Library Cataloguing in Publication Data
Data available

ISBN: 978-0-19-2729330
1 3 5 7 9 10 8 6 4 2

Printed in Great Britain

Paper used in the production of this book is a natural,
recyclable product made from wood grown in sustainable forests.
The manufacturing process conforms to the environmental
regulations of the country of origin.

For Gregory

Danny and Josh
(and Piddle)

They might be twins but they're NOT the same! Josh loves insects, spiders, beetles and bugs. Danny can't stand them. Anything little with multiple legs freaks him out. So sharing a bedroom with Josh can be . . . erm . . . interesting. Mind you, they both love putting earwigs in big sister Jenny's pants drawer . . .

Danny

- **FULL NAME:** Danny Phillips
- **AGE:** 8 years
- **HEIGHT:** Taller than Josh
- **FAVOURITE THING:** Skateboarding
- **WORST THING:** Creepy-crawlies and tidying
- **AMBITION:** To be a stunt man

Josh

- **FULL NAME:** Josh Phillips
- **AGE:** 8 years
- **HEIGHT:** Taller than Danny
- **FAVOURITE THING:** Collecting insects
- **WORST THING:** Skateboarding
- **AMBITION:** To be an entomologist

Piddle

- **FULL NAME:** Piddle the dog Phillips
- **AGE:** 2 dog years
  (14 in human years)
- **HEIGHT:** Not very
- **FAVOURITE THING:** Chasing sticks
- **WORST THING:** Cats
- **AMBITION:** To bite a squirrel

CONTENTS

Horror at the Hedge   11

Call me Petty   21

Bush Ambush   35

Bathroom Soup   45

Snot Funny   55

A Narrow Squeak   65

Happy Snappy   75

Picture Perfect   81

Flying Finish   89

Horror at the Hedge

'Buzz off, you revolting little pest!' Jenny thwacked Danny on the head with her rolled-up magazine.

Josh tried not to giggle. His sister had been reading peacefully for five minutes, unaware that Danny was crouched on the back of the sofa behind her, rubbing the backs of his hands together, poking out his tongue and rolling his eyes madly. A half eaten biscuit in her hand, Jenny hadn't even noticed Josh standing in the doorway, taking pictures with his little digital camera.

It was only when Danny started buzzing that things turned ugly.

'Go and play outside, you creepy little horrors!' yelled Jenny, who was fourteen, so thought she could boss them around. She whacked Danny again and he fell off the sofa and rolled across the sitting room floor, laughing and buzzing.

Josh tucked his camera into his pocket and strolled out towards the front garden with his twin brother. 'Of course, if you *really* wanted to be a fly, you should have spat stomach acid on her Jammy Dodger, walked all over it until it was mush and *then* eaten it.'

Danny biffed the back of Josh's neat fair head as they went down the hallway. 'And Mum says *I'm* the disgusting one!'

'It's just nature,' shrugged Josh, biffing Danny back on his spiky fair head. 'Flies are amazing—I can show you one under my microscope if you like.'

'Yuck! I *don't* like!' shuddered Danny. It was one thing pretending to be an insect to annoy Jenny, but he hated the real thing.

'You ate one quite happily a couple of weeks ago,' Josh reminded him.

Danny stopped dead on the front doorstep. 'I thought we agreed never to talk about that again!'

'Well, yeah, but—'

'NEVER!' said Danny.

Outside, Mum was by the front hedge, talking to Mrs Sharpe from down the road. The garden looked fantastic—carefully trimmed and mown and full of flowers, bushes, and little trees, all overflowing with colourful blossom. The hedge, though, was her real pride and joy. For years she had trimmed and trained it into three little bird shapes along the top. It was a special skill called 'topiary', she had explained to Josh and Danny. She called them her 'hedge birds'.

'Come to help with the weeding, boys?' she asked, when she saw them. Mum had gone in for the Best Garden competition in their village. Last year she'd come third, and this year she was determined to win. Piddle, their terrier dog, had been banned from going anywhere near the front garden. He was shut in the back garden today, out of harm's way.'Can't see any weeds!' said Josh.

'There are some there,' said Mrs Sharpe, pointing at the rose bed. 'And over by the marigolds. Quite a few really. Of course, my garden is completely weed free now—with only one day to go before judging, I couldn't possibly allow anything wild to start messing it up.' She smiled smugly at them all. 'Have to make sure I keep the cup again this year, don't I, Tarquin?'

A thin, pale boy of about Josh and Danny's age slithered around from behind his mother, and gave their garden a look of great disdain. 'I think your trophy is *quite* safe, Mother,' he said, in a high-pitched voice.

'Well,' said Mum, twisting a dead rose bloom off its stalk with some force. 'How nice to have such a

supportive son, Mrs Sharpe.'

'He *is* a darling,' sighed Mrs Sharpe. 'And did I tell you that he scored top in his whole school for maths this week? He's Mummy's little genius!' She patted Tarquin's neatly parted dark hair. 'Of course, not every child can be a genius, can they?' She smiled pityingly at Josh and Danny. 'But that doesn't matter, *does it*?'

Danny made 'being sick' noises and Tarquin pulled ugly faces at them.

'Well, must get on!' Mum knelt down and drove her trowel viciously into the soil. 'We never know *who* might win this year, do we?'

'Don't we?' smirked Mrs Sharpe. 'Well, have fun trying. It really is quite a *nice* little garden . . .' And she stalked off with her son who was still poking his tongue out at Josh and Danny.

'Come on, you two,' said Mum. 'Pay no attention to the genius! Weeding, please!'

Josh and Danny worked their way along the wall, pulling out very tiny weeds and throwing them into Mum's wheelbarrow. 'Weee-aaargh!' shrieked Danny, wildly flapping his hand. A small spider dropped off it and scuttled away.

'You know, I'm surprised you haven't got over your fear of spiders,' said Josh, quietly. 'Considering you've *been* a spider.'

'*DON'T* remind me!' Danny looked around warily for more eight-legged foes. 'I'm trying to forget it ever happened.'

'What—that we got hit by Miss Potts's SWITCH spray? And we got changed into spiders, fell down the bathplug, got rescued by rats, nearly eaten by a toad and a blackbird and then got made human again—all before tea?' Josh grinned as Danny narrowed his eyes at him.

'I don't know *how* you can be so calm about it!' grunted Danny, brutally pulling up a dandelion.

'I'm not!' said Josh. 'It gives me the shivers just to think about Petty Potts, hidden away in her secret lab behind the shed, turning all kinds of poor creatures into bugs just for fun. But it *was* kind of exciting, too—wasn't it? And she *did* turn us back again.'

'Exciting? It was *terrifying*! I was a *spider*! A spider! I was scared of my *own legs*!'

Josh chucked another handful of weeds into the wheelbarrow. 'Well, don't worry. It's all in the past now. We haven't even seen Petty Potts since. And we're *never* going next door again!'

'Ah!' said their mum, to someone at the gate. 'Good timing! I'm just about to go to the garden centre now. Is it still OK for the boys to come round to your house?'

Danny and Josh looked up from their weeding. Their mouths fell open in horror.

Standing by the hedge was their next-door neighbour—Petty Potts.

Call Me Petty

'NOOOOOO!' shouted Josh and Danny, staring, aghast, at the secret scientist who had transformed them into spiders.

'Josh! Danny!' Their mother looked at them crossly. 'How can you be so rude?'

'We—we—we mean . . . ' gabbled Josh. 'We mean we wanted to come along to the garden centre with you. Th-that's all . . . '

Danny just gibbered.

'Well, you can't come! I have a lot to do if I'm going to win the contest. I don't need you two running around and climbing up the trellises!' Mum put her hands on her hips. They knew it was no good arguing when she did that, but Danny tried anyway.

'We could help . . . ' he began.

'No! You couldn't! I would leave you here but Jenny's going out—and Miss Potts has very kindly offered to babysit you. Now, isn't that nice of her?'

Petty Potts smiled sweetly at them. To Danny she looked like a wolf in a tweed hat and glasses. 'Come on in,' she said, heading back to her house. 'I have cake . . . '

'Right,' said their mum. 'Off you go then.'

'But she's . . . weird!' hissed Danny.

'Nonsense,' said their mother. 'She's very nice once you get to know her. I know she was always complaining about your noisy playing before, but just recently I think she's become rather fond of you both.'

'It's only because she wants to use us for experiments,' muttered Danny.

Mum laughed. 'You and your mad ideas, Danny! Now, on your best behaviour, please, both of you. What are you waiting for? She said there's cake!'

'DON'T YOU TRY ANYTHING, MISS POTTS!' warned Josh, the moment Petty Potts's front door closed behind them. Her hallway was dark and old-fashioned and smelt of damp wood.

'Oh, do call me Petty. And stop being such a ninny,' she said. 'I have no intention of wasting good SWITCH spray on you again. I've already tried it on you and it worked. No need to repeat the experiment.'

'Why are you being all nice to Mum, then?' asked Danny, with a suspicious glare.

'I'm just trying to be a good neighbour.' She beckoned them down the hall and into her warm kitchen. There was, indeed, an iced sponge cake on the table, with cups of orange squash next to it. Petty sat down at the table and waved her guests towards two neighbouring chairs. 'But—all right—if you must know, I *have* been wondering

whether your little spider adventure has had any after effects. How have you been?'

'Fine,' grunted Danny, sitting down as Josh took the seat beside him. He eyed the cake, tormented. It looked so good but . . . 'Have you put something in that?' he asked. 'Are you trying to turn us into spiders again?'

Petty stood up and looked at them squarely. 'Now, listen. I know you both think I'm some kind of old witch, but I am merely trying to work on my experiments. I didn't *ask* you to come running into my lab and stand in front of the SWITCH spray jet, did I?'

'No,' said Josh. 'But you *were* trying to spray Piddle!'

'I beg your pardon?' Petty raised an eyebrow behind her spectacles.

'Our dog! Piddle! You were trying to spray *him*, weren't you?'

'All right. Hands up to that,' she said, sitting back down at the table and cutting the cake. 'But let's not bicker about it. It would only have been temporary. I promise I won't try to spray Piddle again—*or* either of you.' She took a big wedge of cake and bit into it. 'Sheee?' she said. 'It'sh quite shafe to eat!'

The cake was too good to resist. After a few bites they started to relax. Petty also sipped from one of their cups of squash to prove these weren't full of SWITCH juice.

'All quite safe. Mind you,' sighed Petty, with a wistful look on her face, 'a little part of me was *hoping . . .*'

'Hoping *what?*' asked Josh, his cake frozen halfway to his mouth.

'No—no it doesn't matter,' said Petty, picking up crumbs by squashing them together on her finger. 'Nothing.'

'*What?*' demanded Danny.

Petty licked the crumbs off her finger and eyed them both as if she was adding something up. 'Well, the fact is, I need help.'

'You're not kidding,' grunted Danny.

'I *meant* I need help with my amazing research,' said Petty. 'I've been working alone for far too long. If I had some assistance . . . well . . . put it this way, we wouldn't just be talking about spiders or ants or flies.' She paused dramatically. 'We'd also be talking about . . . dragons.'

Josh and Danny stared at her.

'Close your mouth, Danny,' said Petty. 'I can see your munched-up cake.'

'Dragons?' echoed Josh. 'You mean you could make us turn into dragons?'

'Doesn't matter, though, does it?' said Petty, briskly cutting another slice of cake. 'Because you

don't want anything to do with the S.W.I.T.C.H.
Project. It's far too dangerous.'

'H-how? How can you turn us into dragons?'
gulped Danny.

'Well, in fact, I can't,' said Petty. 'Not yet. Not
until I've found something which I lost. Once I've
found it, there will be no stopping me! I will work
my way up from insects to reptiles. Maybe even
mammals and birds. But not until I have found it.'

'Found what?' asked Josh.

Petty peered at them hard. 'My memory,' she
said. Josh and Danny peered back at their weird
neighbour, astonished.

'Well, in fact I didn't *lose* it,' she went on. 'It
was destroyed. By Victor Crouch.'

'Victor Crouch? Who's he?' asked Danny. This
was starting to feel like a very odd guessing game.

Petty suddenly drove the cake knife into the
table with a vicious crack.

'Victor Crouch and I used to be good friends.
We both worked for the government—in the best
laboratories in the world, hidden underground
somewhere in Berkshire. That's where I first

stumbled upon the formula to create the SWITCH spray, but I kept the secret to myself. Then Victor discovered my diary, read it, and decided to steal my work!'

She pulled the cake knife out of the table and Danny and Josh flinched as she stabbed it back in again, with even more force. 'So he stole my notes, claimed the S.W.I.T.C.H. Project was all his own work—and then . . . he burnt my memory out and got me fired!'

Josh and Danny gulped. 'How did he burn your memory out?' breathed Danny.

'Oh—there are all kinds of clever ways to do that!' muttered Petty. 'I only know it happened because of my nose.'

'Your nose?' queried Josh.

'Yes—it doesn't work properly any more! And one thing I *do* remember about my old government agency days is that when you burn out part of someone's memory, you mess up their sense of smell too. I can't smell things correctly. This cake smells like cheese. Cheese smells like coal. And so on . . .'

'So how come you're still working on your project then?' asked Josh.

'Well,' grinned Petty, 'what Victor didn't know was that I had *expected* something like this to happen one day! So I transformed all my notes into a secret code—and then I left fake notes in their place, just in case someone ever tried to do the dirty on me! The *real* secret code for each SWITCH spray is chopped into six parts—and each part is hidden inside one of these.' She pulled something from a red velvet box on the table, and held it up to the light. A small cube of glass twinkled in her fingers. Inside it was a hologram of a spider—and some strange symbols in a line beneath it. 'It's a SWITCH formula cube,' she said. 'Inside this one is part of the code for what I call the BUGSWITCH Spray. I have the other five of these—the complete set of BUGSWITCH cubes.' She turned the red velvet box round and they saw five more cubes, glinting in the light through the kitchen window, each with slightly different holograms. 'That's why I can make BUGSWITCH spray.' She pressed the cube into the dent in the box beside the others and snapped the lid shut. 'BUT—there are more! I know there are REPTOSWITCH cubes too! Because I have just one cube in this box—and five empty spaces.' She flipped open the green velvet box and held up another cube—this one with a tiny lizard hologram inside it and more strange symbols.

'And there might be mammal cubes! There may even be bird cubes! I can't be sure. I don't know how far I got before Victor Crouch did a smash and grab on my brain. But first of all, I *have* to find the REPTOSWITCH formula hidden in the missing cubes.'

She rolled the rather beautiful, single REPTOSWITCH cube round in her palm and held it closer to Danny and Josh. 'So . . . if you *were* to become my assistants, and if we were to *find* all the REPTOSWITCH cubes . . . well . . . who's to say you couldn't find out what it's like to be a *dragon*?'

Bush Ambush

Josh and Danny were silent. They gazed at the glass cube with its holographic lizard. 'But,' said Josh, after a while, 'there's no such thing as a dragon. We know you can do spiders—but they're real. Dragons are just make believe.' Josh knew a lot about wildlife. For an eight year old he was really quite an expert and he was quite certain dragons did not exist.

'Well, what about the Komodo dragon?' said Petty.

'OK—there is a Komodo dragon,' admitted Josh.

'And a water dragon,' added Petty.

'Well, yes—all right! But they're just types of lizards,' said Josh. 'They can't fly or breathe fire.'

'But don't you see, Josh?' said Petty. 'I can make humans turn into spiders! Why not go a step further? Mix up a bird formula with the reptile formula? Maybe I could create a DRAGOSWITCH spray too? Wouldn't you like to find out?'

Josh and Danny started to bite their lips and tap their fingers against the table top. It was an amazing idea.

'Oh come on!' urged Petty, putting the cube back into its box. 'You can't tell me you don't want to try out being a dragon one day! And all you have to do is help me find the missing cubes! They can't be far away. I wouldn't have hidden them in Timbuktu! They're bound to be close to my lab. So you could help me look! And maybe try out a few sprays with me . . . I promise you'll be quite safe!'

It was the look on Petty's face which made Josh and Danny stop the finger tapping and lip biting. She looked like a spider herself now, beckoning them into her web.

'No,' said Josh.

'No,' agreed Danny. 'You're nuts!'

Petty opened her mouth.

And then there was a loud, anguished scream. It came from outside. Danny, Josh, and Petty Potts ran down the hallway and were out at the front of the house in seconds. Mum was outside, staring at her hedge.

The lovingly tended hedge birds had been cut off.

'Who would have done such a thing?' gasped Mum, gazing woefully at the mangled stumps of twig which were left. There was no sign of the hedge birds, other than a scattering of their leaves on the pavement.

'Well you don't have to be a genius to work that out,' said Petty Potts. 'Even though I am one. It'll be Mrs Sharpe—or her loathsome son.'

'No!' Mum looked shocked.

'Well, you don't think she keeps winning Best Garden every year by playing fair, do you?' asked Petty. 'Her garden's not that good.'

'But—but how could we ever prove it?' gasped Mum.

'Well, unless you happened to have a camcorder aimed at your garden for the last hour, you can't!' said Petty. She looked at Josh and Danny with a wide, innocent smile. 'If only you could somehow get into their house and be a fly on the wall . . .'

Josh and Danny stared back at her. She wasn't really suggesting . . . ? She didn't really mean . . . ? Did she?

'Shall we go back inside, while your mum phones the police?' asked Petty.

'Thanks, Miss Potts,' sighed Mum. 'But I don't think the police can help now—the judging is tomorrow and it's not even as if I can cheat and wire the birds back on—they're gone! But if you could have Josh and Danny a little longer, I think I need to sit down and have a quiet cup of tea.'

'You didn't really mean that—did you?' demanded Danny as soon as they shut Petty's front door. 'About being a fly on the wall?'

'Now remember,' said Petty, leading them through the kitchen and out into the back garden. 'I told you that I would never spray you with BUGSWITCH again. Funnily enough, I do happen to have the bluebottle house-fly variety all set up to go, right now, but I would never spray it on you.'

Josh and Danny followed her through waist-high weeds, across her garden, and into the shed. 'Or ever make you press the time-delay button which enables you to start the spray and then get yourself inside the special spray tent before it goes off.'

'Don't listen to her! Don't go into her shed!' said Danny, as Josh got a glittery look in his eyes.

Petty stepped into the shed, walked past the rarely used lawnmower, the spade, and the rake, and pushed aside the old sacking on the back wall to reveal a red metal door. She turned the handle.

It opened on to a short flight of dark steps, leading down to a gloomy corridor. Danny couldn't stop Josh following her through.

'But we could get over into Mrs Sharpe's house, though—really easily!' said Josh, as they went

down the corridor, which smelt of old bricks and earth—and other more peculiar scents from a room at the end. 'Her garden backs on to ours. We could fly in through her window, have a look around for evidence, and then get back again in two minutes!'

'But . . . it's so dangerous!' gasped Danny.

'Well, you don't have to come,' said Josh. 'But nobody messes with my mum's hedge and gets away with it! Not if I can help it!'

'Of course, I could never recommend that you come in here,' went on Petty, as they arrived in her lab, which was full of odd machinery, gadgets, and a square tent of plastic sheeting right in the middle. 'Or come into the control booth and hit any of the buttons. That would be the very last thing you would want to do.'

Josh went into the booth after her. It was the size of a large cupboard and lit with the green glow of three computer screens, covered in numbers. In front of the screens was a large control panel and the buttons on it were marked with various creepy-crawly shapes, like those in the BUGSWITCH cubes. He saw the spider button, next to a beetle button, just down from an ant button. Below that was a button with a bluebottle shape on it. A fly. A fly on the wall . . .

Josh didn't waste any time. He hit the button.

There was a sudden humming noise and a blue light came on in the plastic tent. He ran across and pushed inside it through a narrow gap, just as the hissing started and a fine yellow mist sprayed across his legs.

'Josh! What are you doing?' yelled Danny.

'It's OK—it won't take long. Back in two minutes,' said Josh.

Danny slapped his forehead and groaned. He knew he couldn't let Josh go on his own. 'This is such a bad idea!' he muttered, and stepped into the tent with his brother.

'Oh my. What have you done?' said Petty, cheerfully. 'Now, remember, it's only temporary— you'll need to get back fast. You don't want to revert to boys while you're still in Mrs Sharpe's house.'

Josh began to feel peculiar. The plastic sheets around him swished into a whirly pattern and then shot upwards, as if he was falling. Yet he could still feel the concrete floor under his two feet. Ah—no. Scratch that. Under his six feet.

Bathroom Soup

'WAHAAAAAY!' shouted Josh. Danny towered
above him like a giant. His nearby foot, in its
muddy trainer, was the size of a truck. Josh seemed
to be looking through thousands of little hexagonal
lenses—and he could see all around him without
even moving. He was bug-eyed!

'WHEEEEE-RRRRE IIIIIIIIIZZZZZ HEEEEEEEEE?'
he heard Danny bellow in a deep loud voice that
vibrated right through his highly tuned black body.

Josh felt his six feet move off the floor and
realized that the ticklish feeling on his back was
coming from the whirring of his own two wings.

'WEEE-HEEE!' he gurgled, full of excitement,
as he rose up in the air like a Harrier jump jet.
A moment later, he was staring, amazed, into
Danny's huge face, his own blue-black body

reflected in the two gigantic shiny orbs of his brother's eyes. His new bluebottle head was almost triangular in shape, but his immense bulging golden eyes softened the corners. Two tiny stubby feelers (called palps, he knew, from his wildlife books) wiggled where his nose used to be, with little spiky antennae on each. Josh stuck out his tongue—but what emerged from his chin area was a black stick-like thing, which bent in the middle, like an elbow. A spongy blob was on the end.

'Woo-hoo!' shouted Josh. 'I've got a proboscis!'

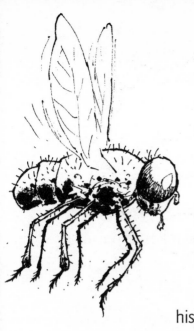

'JOOOOOO-OOOO-OOOSH?' boomed Danny's humungous face, its eyes crinkling up in wonder. And then Danny disappeared into a tiny dot, way down on the floor. A few seconds later he was up in the air next to Josh.

'Josh! Josh!' he squeaked, his bug eyes bulging with amazement. 'I can fly!'

'It's a buzz, isn't it?' giggled Josh, flicking his peculiar mouth parts about with excitement.

'And I can see my own bum!' marvelled Danny. 'Without turning my head round!'

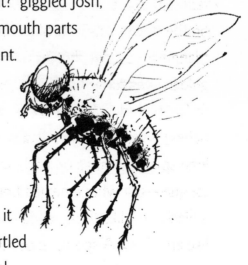

'Well, that makes it all worthwhile!' chortled Josh. 'It's your special fly eyes! They're designed so you can see all the way round, in case of predators. Now! We have to hurry. Follow me—I know the way to Mrs Sharpe's house.'

He could just make out Petty slowly waving a huge pink hand at them as he shot out through the gap in the plastic tent. He flew past the open lab door, back up the steps to the shed and out into Petty's garden, with Danny just behind him. It didn't look so much like a garden now—more like an immense jungle with a tangled mass of exotic trees spreading below them as far as their bug eyes could see. The jungle sent up intense smells of greenery, flower pollen, and something gorgeously brown and sticky from the other side of the fence—near Piddle's basket.

Danny whirled about in astonishment—the sky was filled with aircraft, thundering, thudding, zooming, and whining past. 'It's an air show!' he yelped, dodging what looked like a small black and yellow helicopter with a terrifying face. Two blue jets darted past so fast he got spun around in mid-air.

'Where did all these aircraft come from?'

'They're not aircraft, you dingbat!' said Josh, hovering up alongside him, his dangly black forelegs blowing in the breeze. 'They're other insects. Mind out for the black and yellow ones— they're wasps. They'd happily eat us if they could. The dragonflies—those blue jets—can be pretty fierce too, but I think they're just looking for girlfriends.'

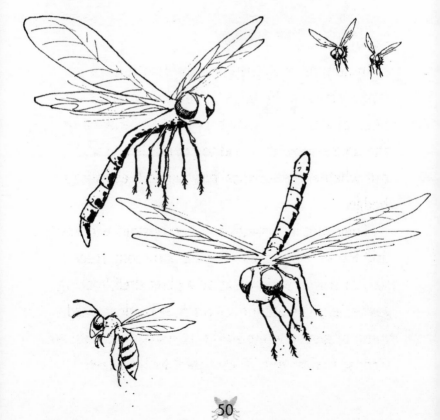

Josh pivoted in the air like an expert pilot and zoomed off towards some giant trees at the end of the garden. Danny followed. Being a fly felt amazing!

'I can't believe I ever thought flies were rubbish!' he called to Josh as he zoomed up behind him and looped the loop. 'They're brilliant!' He felt rather guilty at the brilliant flying machine he had pulped against the bedroom wall with a rolled up comic just last week. And even guiltier about the one he ate when he was a spider.

In no time at all they were across the back fence, between the huge tree trunks, and over Mrs Sharpe's neat and pretty back garden, heading for the house. Now they had to get inside and find out whether the Sharpes' had ruined their mum's hedge.

They shot in through an open upstairs window and found themselves in a vast bathroom. Huge vats of smelly potions sat on a glass shelf, making Josh's sensitive antennae twitch. A boulder-sized lump of greeny-white stuff on the basin sent up an intense minty whiff. Toothpaste! Josh realized.

'Everything smells ten times stronger, doesn't it?' he shouted to Danny. 'Danny? Oh—yuck! Danny! Stop that!' shouted Josh.

Danny jumped and rose up with a shudder.

'You weren't really going to drink that, were you?' asked Josh.

'No—of course not!' spluttered Danny. 'I—I didn't realize I was on the edge of the toilet, did I? I didn't know what it was . . . It just smelt . . . '

'Kind of . . . tasty?' muttered Josh. 'Like bathroom soup.'

Danny pivoted round in the air to stare at his brother. 'It's because we're flies, isn't it?'

'Yep,' said Josh. 'To a fly, wee is soup.'

'And that really nice smell from near Piddle's basket . . . ?'

'Let's just get going, shall we?' said Josh, briskly. 'We've got work to do!'

They flew around the edge of the bathroom door and dropped through the warm updraught of air from downstairs. Now they could hear voices—heavy, slow, and human.

Following the voices, which vibrated around them, they arrived in the kitchen. It smelt incredibly sweet. Mrs Sharpe was making cakes. Tarquin was with her, sitting at the kitchen table.

'Shhh!' said Josh. 'Let's wait here and listen for a while—see if they own up to chopping up Mum's hedge . . .'

And then the room flipped over.

Snot Funny

It didn't seem strange that the room had flipped over. To Josh and Danny, now standing on the ceiling, being upside down felt like the most natural thing in the world.

'This is so cool!' said Danny. 'And ooooh, that cake mix smells so good!'

'Sshh! We need to listen to them!' said Josh. It wasn't easy, because just like the last time, when they'd shrunk into spiders, human speech sounded much deeper and slower than usual. After a while, though, Josh felt his quick fly brain adapt and he began to understand what Mrs Sharpe and Tarquin were saying.

'Good work, Tarquin,' said Mrs Sharpe. 'Are you sure nobody saw you?'

'Of course not, Mother!' sniffed Tarquin. 'I am not an idiot, you know!'

'Good—just as long as you're sure. Even though my garden is obviously the best in town, the judge could have been charmed by those dreadful tacky topiary birds. Now there's not much chance of that! Did you hide them, like I said. I wouldn't put it past her to cheat and wire them back on.'

'Yes, Mother—they're in the front room.'

Josh and Danny gasped. Petty was right!

'The front room? Are you mad? What if the judge calls in early and finds the evidence all over the carpet?' Mrs Sharpe waved her wooden spoon around in fury and a large blob of cake mix splodged onto the floor. A wonderful scent hit Danny like a wave and he just couldn't help himself. He dropped down from the ceiling, turning a somersault in the air, and buzzed straight for the floor.

'Danny!' called Josh. 'We haven't got time for snacks! We have to find Mum's hedge birds!'

'I can't . . . help . . . myself . . . ' wailed back Danny, landing on the pale yellow blob, which rose up like a small hill from the red floor tile. His proboscis stuck out of his face and squelched down into the glorious squidgy mess.

Something gooey shot out of the end of it, making the cake mix go squishier still, so he could suck it up like a milkshake. Ooooooooooh! It was lovely!

Josh landed beside Danny with a plop. 'Come on,' he said. 'Time to go!' But before he could say another word, his own proboscis had shot out and was busy spitting goo out too. A second later, Josh was also sucking up cake mix and fly-spit smoothie.

Then there was a sudden whoosh of wind
behind them and a terrifying thrumming noise.
Josh and Danny looked up to see a huge orange
criss-cross square hurtling towards them.

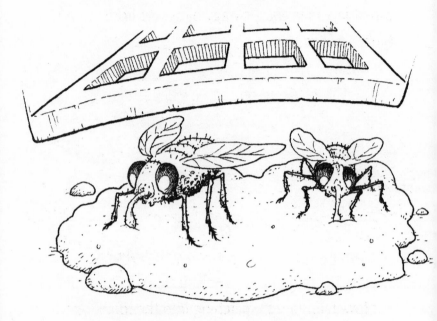

'ARRRGH!' yelled Danny, shooting high into
the air, his proboscis snapping back into his face
like a pinged rubber band. 'It's a fly swat! They're
swatting us!' Josh had worked this out too. He
zoomed across the kitchen so fast his vision
blurred. Danny flew close behind him, yelling,
'GO! GO! GO! GO!'

A second later they were in the hallway and
then Josh turned left and flew into the front room.
'Look!' he yelled, angrily, pointing with one of
his front legs. There on the vast field of swirly red
carpet lay three leafy, twiggy birds, cut from
Mum's hedge.

Now Tarquin was marching into the room with
Mrs Sharpe at his heels. She still held the fly swat.
Tarquin had a bin bag in his hand.

'Pick them up then,' said Mrs Sharpe. 'No—
wait—we'll have to pull them to pieces first, just in
case the bin men spot them.'

And she went to pick up Mum's favourite hedge
bird creation.

'NOOOOOOOOOOOOO!' yelled Josh and dive-bombed Mrs Sharpe's face. He aimed for her nose—a huge pink outcrop on the massive pink slab of her face—and before he could rethink the idea, had shot right up her left nostril.

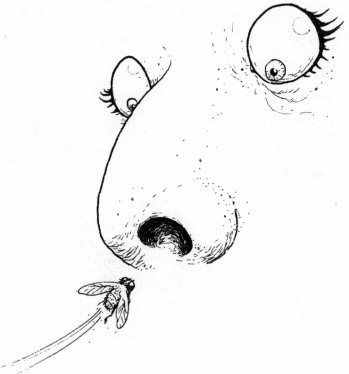

It certainly distracted her. As Josh rolled over in the nasty, draughty, hairy cavern, Mrs Sharpe shrieked and spluttered and sneezed—and Josh hurtled back out again in a blast of nose goo.

He ended up stuck to the leather sofa in a green globule. Danny, meanwhile, flew down and shot under the sofa. He zoomed low over the thick clumps of dust and hair and the twisted sculptures of sweet wrappers on the shadowy carpet. He aimed for the line of light at the far side, planning to shoot quickly up the back of the sofa and get hold of Josh from behind. He didn't want to attract the fly swat which Tarquin was now twitching about in the air. But just a few centimetres up the back of the sofa, something pushed hard against Danny's head, stopping him in flight.

It felt as if he'd flown into goal during a football match. Like a big net. A big, sticky, net. A big, sticky, shivering net . . . Danny shouted and tried to get back down off the net, but it stuck to him like . . . like . . . like . . . A WEB!

In the dusty darkness, eight red eyes suddenly lit up. Eight long, hairy legs began to pick their way down the silken ropes towards Danny.

Danny didn't know as much about wildlife as Josh did, but he knew this much—the spider was coming to meet him for lunch.

And Danny was on the menu!

A Narrow Squeak

Josh had just managed to slither out of the giant bogey and edge away over the back of the sofa when he heard Danny scream. He could only just hear it over Mrs Sharpe, who was still sneezing and gasping and blowing her nose noisily. Josh peered down from the top of the sofa and saw a terrifying sight.

A huge hairy spider was flipping Danny over and over with its legs and wrapping him up in silk. Danny was struggling hard, but he was no match for the spider—a female, judging by her size and skinny palps, thought Josh.

'Look!' he shouted down. 'This is all a mistake! He's not actually a fly at all and nor am I!' The spider paused, looked up at Josh, narrowed all eight eyes, and then came running for him, obviously fancying him as pudding.

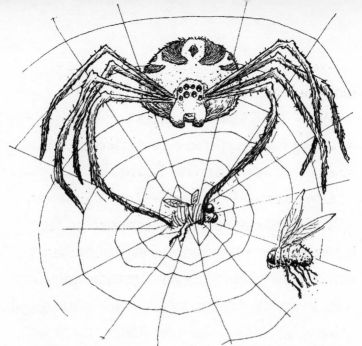

'Fly away!' called up Danny, in a rather muffled way. Several bands of silk were across his face. Josh did, whizzing up out of reach. Then the spider scuttled back down to her main course.

'It's all right, Danny,' yelled down Josh, hovering above. 'She won't kill you right away . . . she'll just . . . um . . . bite you . . . a bit . . . '

'A bit?' squawked Danny.

'Yeah . . . and paralyse you with her venom . . . and . . . '

'And?' mumbled Danny, through a mouthful of silk. 'And what?'

'Well . . . then she'll wait till your insides go runny before eating you.'

'Well—thanks for that!' called back Danny. 'Knowing exactly what to expect makes me feel so much better!'

'Don't worry—I'll rescue you!' called back Josh.

'Will you?' queried Danny, as the lady spider lowered her brown and grey speckly face towards him, and slid a pair of fat fangs out of her mouth parts.

'No.'

'Ah.' Danny shut his eyes.

'But they will!'

There was a crunching noise.

Danny opened his eyes just in time to see the spider's last leg disappearing into the furry face of . . .

'SCRATCH!' he yelled, joyfully. 'SNIFF!' he added, just as joyfully, as another furry face appeared. Two giant brown rats were now peering at him with great concern. The last time he and Josh had met Scratch and Sniff, the rats had saved their lives. It looked as if it was becoming a habit!

'Careful now,' said Scratch. 'It's pretty delicate
work, picking silk off a fly without picking the legs
off with it. Normally we just eat flies still wrapped.'

Danny hiccuped in fright. 'Oh, don't be daft—
I'm windin' you up,' laughed Scratch. 'We don't
eat flies. We and flies have a bond! Humans hate
'em as much as us! And all rats and flies do is tidy
things up, you know—clear up the gooey stuff
that you don't want lying around. Nah. We get
on all right, rats and flies. Want me to get a swarm
together and have them attack that Petty Potts for
you? Ow—this stuff
is sticky!'

'Oh, move
over! Let me!'
said his wife.

Sniff leaned over and carefully began to unwind the
silk with her delicate, long-nailed fingers.

Josh landed next to them. 'You scoffed that spider
in one munch!' he marvelled. 'I thought you two
said you never ate spiders . . . the last time we met.'

'Well, dear,' said Sniff, still carefully unravelling
Danny. 'We were being polite. You were both
spiders yourselves at the time.'

'Don't really like 'em much,' said Scratch, picking
a bit of thorax out of his teeth with a cough. 'But
can't have one of 'em eating an old friend, can we?'

'What are you both doing here?' asked Josh.

'Oh, just doing our rounds, love,' said Sniff.

'Always worth popping in when she's making

cakes. She drops a lot of mixture. We came in and heard a bit of a to-do in here, and we recognized your voices!'

'Thank you so much!' sighed Josh. 'I thought Danny was done for this time.'

'Well, he will be, if you hang around here much longer,' said Scratch, casting his beady eyes around the dark cave behind the sofa. 'Plenty more spiders where that one came from. How come you let that mad scientist catch you and spray you again?'

'We didn't—I mean—we decided to spray ourselves, this time,' said Danny, getting back up on his six feet and carefully flexing his wings.

'You must be stark staring bonkers,' said Sniff, shaking her head with a quiver of whiskers. 'You nearly got eaten last time—and here you are nearly getting eaten again! Didn't you learn your lesson?'

Danny and Josh quickly explained their mission.

'So,' said Scratch, 'let me get this straight. You let Petty Potts turn you into flies so you could rescue some bits of twig for your mum?'

'Well . . . sort of,' said Josh. He had to admit that it now seemed like a fairly silly idea. 'We wanted to find out if it really was Mrs Sharpe or Tarquin that cut the twigs off—and now we've found them here, Mum might still be able to wire the twigs back on again if we can get them back.'

'What—those bits of twigs that they're picking up and pulling apart now?' checked Scratch.

'NO!' shouted Josh and Danny, together.

'You've got to stop them! Please!' begged Josh. 'We're too tiny to make any difference! Can you both create a distraction?'

Scratch and Sniff looked at each other, shrugged, and then ran out across the carpet.

'Eeeeek, eeeeek,' said Scratch in a rather bored voice as Mrs Sharpe whirled around, looked down, and began to shriek with horror. 'Eee-eek. Look at me. I might be carrying the plague . . .'

He and his wife disappeared into the hallway, calling back, 'Come on! Eeeeeek! Chase us!'

'How many times must I tell you,' they heard Sniff scold him, 'not to keep bringing up the plague?'

With much squealing, and hand flapping, Mrs Sharpe and Tarquin ran out after them.

Josh and Danny grinned at each other and then flew up away from the dusty dark cave behind the sofa. From high up on the ceiling they could see the hedge birds still lying on the floor; only one of them had lost a wing.

'Let's fly back, get Petty to de-bug us, and then bring Mum round here fast to confront them, before they have time to destroy the evidence!' said Danny.

'OK,' said Josh. 'If we can ever get Mum to believe us.'

Danny zoomed across the room and out into the hallway but Josh suddenly felt rather peculiar and heavy. One moment he was in the air, about to fly after his twin brother—the next . . .

72

Josh found himself face down on the swirly
red carpet. He had just changed back into a boy!
He sprang up and opened his mouth to shout to
Danny, but then realized that he couldn't—he was
in Mrs Sharpe's front room! She and Tarquin were
just outside in the hall squawking about Scratch
and Sniff.

'Let's get the poker and the coal tongs from the
fire. We can beat them out with those!' shrieked
Mrs Sharpe.

And the sitting room door was flung open.

Happy Snappy

Josh hurled himself back behind the sofa—a much tighter fit this time—just as they walked in.

'Ugh! How disgusting!' shuddered Mrs Sharpe. 'We shall have to call in the council—but how can we? The neighbours will see and I will be so humiliated. Imagine—rats! Vermin in my home— my garden!'

Josh stared through a narrow gap between the sofa and the wall and watched them crouch down by the hedge birds. There was a whimpering noise.

'Oh for heaven's sake!' snapped Mrs Sharpe. 'Stop crying, Tarquin!'

'But, Mother! One of them scratched me when I tried to kick it. I might have caught the Black Death,' sniffed Tarquin.

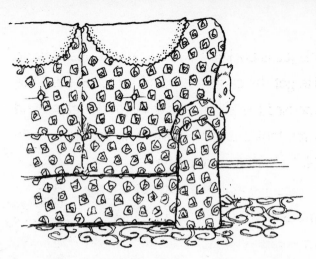

'For a genius, you really are an oaf, Tarquin!' was his mother's tender reply.

Jammed behind the sofa, Josh wondered what to do next. The evidence of cheating in the Best Garden Contest was right in front of him—but now he was trapped! The window was just above his head, but if he tried to escape through it Mrs Sharpe and Tarquin would see him. They could call the police and then hide the evidence of their own crime before the police arrived. Even with Danny backing him up, who was going to believe two eight year olds against Mrs Sharpe and her son?

And where was Danny?

This was not going to plan. Not at all. Josh sighed. Then he felt something digging through

his jeans pocket. His new camera! Josh grinned.
He got the camera out and switched it on. He
focused the zoom lens through the gap—and
then took a picture of Mrs Sharpe and her son.
Not a very flattering one . . .

'It's like a plague in here!'
muttered Mrs Sharpe. 'First flies,
then rats—whatever next?
A swarm of locusts?' Just as
she reached for Mum's favourite
hedge bird her eyes widened and she paused.

'What was that clicking noise?'

'Locusts?' breathed Tarquin, looking scared.

'It came from behind the sofa!' she whispered,
and mother and son turned to stare right at the
spot where Josh was hidden. He could see them
through the gap, but could they see him?

'Tarquin—go and look behind the sofa!' ordered
Mrs Sharpe.

'But—I don't want to!' wailed Tarquin. 'It might
be more rats . . . '

'If you want any tea today, you'll do as you're
told!' snapped his mother.

Tarquin crept towards the sofa, curled his bony fingers across the top of it, and pulled. Josh cringed. He was about to be found out, skulking behind the furniture in a neighbour's house, like a burglar.

'AAAARGH!' screamed Mrs Sharpe. 'RATS! RATS! THERE THEY GO AGAIN.'

Josh laughed silently with relief. Scratch and Sniff had run into the room, done a loop around the carpet and run off out again.

As soon as Mrs Sharpe and Tarquin had hurried out after them, Josh leapt to his feet, jumped over the sofa, gathered Mum's hedge birds into the bin bag, slung it over his shoulder and then climbed through the front room window. He landed on the immaculate front lawn. With Mrs Sharpe's screams and Tarquin's shrieks echoing from the house, he ran for the gate and made straight for home.

As he reached the corner of the road, he ran right into Danny.

'There you are!' cried his brother. 'We thought you'd been swatted!'

Petty could be seen hurrying along the road

behind Danny. 'Oh, thank goodness!' she puffed.
'You've not been eaten! Now—you naughty
boys—don't ever do such a thing ever again!'

Josh and Danny turned and gave her a very
hard stare.

'Oh, all right,' she muttered, adjusting her
spectacles. 'I just like to pretend to be a
normal grown-up sometimes . . .'

Picture Perfect

The camera memory stick slid into Petty's computer, which clicked and whirred.

'It's very powerful, but a bit slow,' said Petty, in the green light of the laboratory.

'Um . . . one thing I've been wondering about . . . ' ventured Danny.

'Yes, Danny?' said Petty, pushing her glasses up her nose and jabbing at the keyboard.

'Why aren't I stark naked?'

Petty blinked in surprise. 'Because it's a little chilly today?'

'No—I mean why aren't there a couple of piles of clothes in the plastic tent thingy where we got SWITCHed?' went on Danny. 'When we turned into flies we should have flown right out of our pants, shouldn't we? And then when we came back to being human, we should've been stark naked!'

Petty laughed. 'A good point, Danny. It's to do with how SWITCH works. It actually changes all your cells' energy patterns—and everything that's connected to them at the point when you are sprayed gets changed too.'

'Energy patterns?' repeated Josh.

'Yes. All you need to know is that everything immediately connected to you changes with you. OK?'

Josh and Danny nodded, slowly.

'And a jolly good thing too,' added Petty. 'A pair of identical streaking eight year olds is the last thing we need when we're working together on a top secret project.'

'Are we . . . ?' said Danny, looking at Josh. 'Working on a top secret project? With her?'

Josh shrugged. He hadn't decided yet. No matter how exciting it was to think of being a dragon one day, it was just so dangerous. Only an hour ago, Danny had nearly been a spider's lunch!

There was a ping.

'Ah!' said Petty. 'Here are your photos, Josh.'

A series of photos opened up across her large screen. Josh's finger. Josh's eye. Danny, his head sideways, laughing hard at Josh for trying to take a photo with his new camera back to front and skew-whiff. Then pictures of Mum in the garden, a close up of the rockery, Danny pretending to be a giant fly, sitting up behind Jenny's shoulder, Jenny hitting him with her rolled up magazine . . .

And then, three really clear shots of . . .

. . . a swirly red carpet.

'What?' squawked Josh. 'Oh no! Where's Mrs Sharpe and Tarquin? Now we've got no evidence!'

'You must have messed up the angle,' muttered Danny. 'What a waste of time!'

'Nonsense,' said Petty Potts, leaning in close to peer at the photos. 'You got the hedge birds back for your mum, didn't you?'

'Yes, but I wanted the police to go round and arrest Mrs Sharpe and Tarquin!' huffed Josh.

Petty had maximized one photo on her computer so it filled the whole screen, and was now peering so closely at it that her nose was against the monitor. 'Who cares about them?' she said, with growing excitement in her voice. 'Josh! Where is this?' and she jabbed her finger at the picture of Mum's rockery. Josh noticed, for the first time, that something bright was shining under one of the rocks. Probably a bit of broken bottle.

'I took that in the front garden,' said Josh. Why?'

'Take me there! Right away!' demanded Petty, springing to her feet. Josh and Danny shrugged at each other and led the way. Two minutes later Petty Potts was on her hands and knees, scrabbling

through the rockery. It was a good thing Mum
had gone inside after wiring the hedge birds back
on. She would have been horrified. But after just
a few seconds, Petty leapt to her feet and held up
something covered in dirt. 'YESS!' she cried.
'Look! Josh! Danny! I can't believe it!'

They stared closely at the thing in her hand
and some of the loose dirt fell away from it. It was
a glass cube.

'Wow—it's—it's one of those SWITCH cube
thingies!' breathed Danny.

Now he could see a holographic image inside the glass. It looked a bit like an alligator.

Petty Potts held the cube to her cheek. 'Another REPTOSWITCH cube! I knew they couldn't be far away! I knew it. Now . . . if only I could remember where I'd hidden the rest.'

'Are you sure you hid them?' said Josh.

'Yes—my memory is burnt out in places, as you know, but I remember hiding the cubes where I could find them later in an emergency. There are another four of these—the REPTOSWITCH ones— hidden somewhere near the lab,' explained Petty.

'Except you forgot where,' pointed out Danny.

'Yes! Exactly! So far, I've only managed to find the cubes with the BUGSWITCH code. All the others have been lost for years! And that's why I need your help. Will you look for REPTOSWITCH cubes for me?' asked Petty, smiling at them hopefully (and less like a spider in a web this time).

'Look,' said Josh. 'We will help you—we will look for your cubes. But we won't change into any more bugs. OK?'

'Absolutely fine!' said Petty. 'I would never dream of asking you to.'

She put the glass cube in her pocket and put her rather muddy fingers on each of their heads.

'Josh—Danny. Welcome to the SWITCH Project!'

Flying Finish

'Well, this is lovely, I must say!' The Best Garden
judge smiled approvingly at the garden.
'I particularly like these!' he added, patting the
hedge birds. 'They must have taken years to grow
and cut into such delightful shapes.' Around the
judge, the crowd murmured, impressed.

'Oh yes—years,' agreed Mum, smiling back,
nervously. 'But I have to admit to you that
yesterday somebody came along and chopped
them off. I had to wire them back on.'

The crowd gasped and the judge's eyebrows
rose up. 'They won't last, of course,' went on
Mum. 'In a week the leaves will have died, but
for now they look fine. I hope it won't mean
I'm disqualified, but I'd rather not pretend.' She
was still amazed that the hedge birds had been

returned—Josh and Danny had run into the house to tell her that the hedge birds were lying on the garden path yesterday afternoon.

'Well—I think it's very good of you to be so honest,' said the judge. 'I certainly won't disqualify you over someone else's nasty trick.'

The crowd walked on and Mum, Josh, and Danny walked on with it, watching as the judge inspected other gardens in the competition.

Petty Potts suddenly arrived behind Josh and Danny. They smiled at her, glumly. How they wished Josh's photo of Mrs Sharpe and Tarquin with the hedge birds had come out. They'd spent all morning grumbling about it, sitting by the shed in the back garden—even when Scratch and Sniff had shown up (they lived under the shed) and sat on their shoulders for a while. The rats shook their furry little heads when Josh told them what had happened. 'I can't stand to think of that stuck up Mrs Sharpe winning the prize!' said Danny. Scratch and Sniff squeaked at each other and then vanished back under the shed just as Mum came down the garden to tell Josh and Danny the judging was starting.

Now the crowd gathered at Mrs Sharpe's garden while the judge walked around it.

'You know, I don't think you really wanted to get the police involved, anyway,' Petty muttered. 'After all, they would have wondered how you came to be inside the Sharpes' house. It's for the best.'

Mrs Sharpe's garden was very neat with carefully arranged plants and flowers, a perfect lawn, and a water feature with a little fountain. Mrs Sharpe stood at her gate, wearing a wide-brimmed hat, waving white-gloved hands and nodding at everyone, as if she was the Queen.

'Very good, as usual, Mrs Sharpe,' beamed the judge, after looking around for a few minutes. 'Always one of our star gardens. Quite immaculate.'

'Well, you know I cannot bear untidiness or unpleasantness in a garden,' simpered Mrs Sharpe. 'For me, there has to be perfect order. Nothing less.' Tarquin stood behind her, wearing a neat navy-blue suit and a smug smile.

'Well,' said the judge. 'As this is our last garden, I think I can now announce the winner.'

An expectant hush fell upon the crowd, broken only by the buzzing of a few flies. Then a few more flies. And a bit more buzzing.

The judge fanned his face. 'Gosh! Your garden is a haven for insect life, Mrs Sharpe.'

'Well—butterflies and bees, of course,' trilled Mrs Sharpe, swiping something off her chin.

'No—bluebottles and cluster flies,' said Josh. He grinned. There were a lot of flies. Really quite a swarm in fact. Someone gave a little scream. There were now clouds of flies all over Mrs Sharpe's garden, settling on her neat borders and dancing around her little fountain.

'They're attracted to rubbish, old meat, dog poo—that kind of stuff,' Josh cheerily informed the crowd.

'I don't have rubbish or old meat or dog poo in my garden!' exclaimed Mrs Sharpe.

'Well, you must have. You've certainly got vermin!' pointed out Petty. And there—running around the fountain—were Scratch and Sniff.

They raced up and down the lawn, squeaking, and swirling cyclones of flies followed them.

As the crowd turned panicky, Josh and Danny were doubled up laughing. Scratch and Sniff had obviously decided to help out, after hearing Josh and Danny's bad news earlier.

'Of course!' Josh giggled, wildly, to Danny and Petty. 'Scratch told us he could get flies to swarm for him—now he's proved it!'

Everyone was now edging quickly away from Mrs Sharpe's garden.

'Wait! Wait!' she squealed after them, swatting flies off her clothes in mad swoops. 'I've laid on tea! I've made cakes! Scones and jam . . . to celebrate my victory . . . '

'Nothing to celebrate this year, Mrs Sharpe,' called back the judge, scribbling on his clipboard as he ran down the road. 'You came ninth! Better get the council in for those rats!'

'But I don't have rats! I don't!' sobbed Mrs Sharpe, twitching and dancing while Tarquin slapped his face repeatedly.

Josh stayed long enough to take a photograph. He got the angle right this time.

'Good old Scratch and Sniff!' cheered Danny as their furry friends disappeared behind Mrs Sharpe's greenhouse.

Back at their house, Mum was being cheered by the crowd. She'd won! Even Jenny came outside to join in the celebration.

'Ugh! Flies! How disgusting!' she squealed,
when she heard about the drama. 'I bet Danny
freaked out.'

'Nope,' said Danny. 'Flies are brilliant. I will
never squash a fly again. Flies are my friends.' He
wandered off as Petty sidled up to Josh.

'So—are you both quite all right?' she checked,
peering at him closely. 'No after effects?'

'Not me,' said Josh. He pointed at Danny. 'Not
so sure about him though . . .'

Danny's nose twitched as he stared longingly
at the bin, dribbling.

'Danneeeeee!' called Josh.

'I—can't—help—it . . .' wailed Danny, running
his hands over the lid.

'SPIDER!' shouted Josh and Danny hurtled off
the bin and ran into the house. He nearly collided
with Jenny as she walked back towards the house.

'Oh why must you always bug me?' yelled
Jenny. 'And what are you doing over there, Josh?'

'Um . . . nothing,' said Josh, sniffing at the bin
lid. He ran after Danny before he could give in to
the urge to lick the gooey bits. 'Gotta fly!'

DIARY ENTRY *575.3

SUBJECT: JOSH AND DANNY PHILLIPS—RECRUITMENT

Good work! Have convinced Josh and Danny to join me in the S.W.I.T.C.H. Project—and they don't seem to have suffered any bad side effects from their latest SWITCH, apart from wanting to eat out of dustbins.

Josh is the cleverest one and really knows his wildlife, so he should be quite a help in making notes. Danny is bright too, though, and very brave, considering he is actually quite scared of bugs and insects.

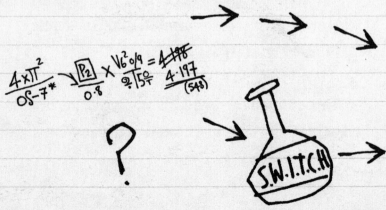

Of course, most importantly, they are four extra eyes in the search for the missing REPTOSWITCH cubes. We found one today! Now I have two out of six. If Josh and Danny can help me find the other four, I will be able to advance the project to the reptilian level!

I haven't told them the whole story, yet.

They know about Victor Crouch—the rotten thief—but they don't know that I think he may be watching me. That's the main reason I can't search too hard for the REPTOSWITCH cubes myself, of course. If Victor, or one of his spies, sees me looking, they will realize that there are more cubes, and start looking too. But Josh and Danny can search the whole street! Because none of Victor's spies will ever suspect two eight-year-old boys, will they?

REPTOSWITCH! HERE WE COME!

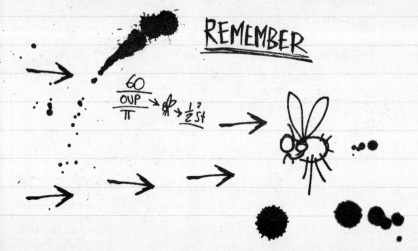

REMEMBER

Glossary

Antennae—Long, thin feelers, protruding from an insect's forehead. Flies use their antennae to smell and feel their surroundings.

Bluebottle—A type of fly with a metallic blue and green thorax. Bluebottles are covered in black bristly hairs. They make a noisy buzzing sound when they fly and are about 10–14 mm long.

Cellular—Something made from a group of living cells.

Hexagonal—A shape that has six sides.

Hijack—To take control of something by force.

Hologram—A picture made up of laser beams which appear three dimensional (3D).

Insect—Animals with six legs and three body parts; the head, thorax, and abdomen.

Locusts—Insects that breed very quickly and fly in large groups called swarms. A swarm of locusts can cause a lot of damage to crops.

Mammal—Animals that give birth to live young and feed them with their own milk. Humans and rats are mammals.

Glossary

Palps—Feelers which spiders use to search for food.

Plague—Sometimes known as the Black Death, the plague was a serious illness. Fleas living on rats carried the disease and spread it to humans.

Proboscis—A long sucking organ or mouth part. Flies use their proboscis to suck up food.

Reptiles—Cold-blooded animals. Lizards and snakes are reptiles.

Thorax—The section of an insect's body between the head and abdomen.

Topiary—Pruning (or trimming) bushes and hedges into attractive shapes.

Vermin—Animals or insects that can damage crops or carry disease. Rats are often described as vermin.

PLACES TO VISIT

Want to brush up on your bug knowledge?
Here's a list of places with areas dedicated
to creepy-crawlies:

Liverpool Museum

http://www.liverpoolmuseums.org.uk/wml/naturalworld/
bughouse/

Marwell Wildlife Park

http://www.marwell.org.uk/

Natural History Museum

http://www.nhm.ac.uk/

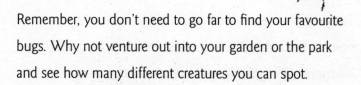

Remember, you don't need to go far to find your favourite
bugs. Why not venture out into your garden or the park
and see how many different creatures you can spot.

WEBSITES

Find out more about nature and wildlife
using the websites below.

http://www.bbc.co.uk/cbbc/wild/
http://www.nhm.ac.uk/kids-only/
http://kids.nationalgeographic.com/
http://switch-books.co.uk/

Another exciting adventure awaits . . .

Ali Sparkes
Winner of the Blue Peter
Book of the Year

Illustrated by
Ross Collins

S.W.I.T.C.H.
SERUM WHICH INSTIGATES TOTAL CELLULAR HIJACK

Grasshopper Glitch

Twitchy Travellers

Danny was jumpy.

'Stop making that *noise*!' snapped Josh as they waited at the gate. Danny was making a peculiar screechy-scrapey noise through his teeth. He was trying to learn to whistle but he only managed to sound like a rusty bike chain being repeatedly dragged against a tin tray.

He didn't pay Josh any attention.

'Will you *stop* it!' Josh whacked his lunchbox against the back of Danny's head and his twin glared at him, rubbing his spiky blond hair.

'I can't help it. I'm nervous!' Danny muttered, eyeing the car at the roadside. The car which would take them to school this morning. Mum couldn't drive them in today and so their next-door neighbour, Petty Potts, was giving them a lift. She was just getting her bag from the house and soon they would be away.

Josh stared at the car too, and felt that his brother had some cause to be jumpy. Petty's car was so old it was actually made of *wood*. The back half of it looked like a chunk of old boat and the dark-green leather seats inside were like furniture from a museum. Piddle, their terrier dog, was cocking his leg against one of the back wheels.

'It can't be legal to drive this around on proper roads!' hissed Danny, as Petty emerged from her gate with a large open-topped woven straw bag in her hands. 'I mean—do you think she's even got a licence?'

'Come along, you two. Hop in,' said Petty, opening the door and tipping up the front passenger seat so they could get into the back. 'Oh, get away from my tyres, you nasty leaky creature!' She glared at Piddle and he grinned up at her doggily before shooting back into the garden and up the side passage where they heard Mum shutting the gate.

Petty tutted and went round to the driver's door. She was in her brown raincoat and wearing her usual tweedy hat, pulled down low over her spectacles. She looked exactly like someone should look, driving such an ancient wreck, thought Danny. 'Pooh.' He pulled a face at Josh as they clambered in across the bouncy cracked leather seat. It also smelt like a museum.

'Where are the seatbelts?' asked Josh looking left and right.

'It's a Morris Traveller, Josh,' said Petty, grinding the gears as the engine coughed into life. 'They didn't build them with seatbelts back in 1966. Just hang on tight—I'm not going to crash.' She turned around, put her bag in between them on the seat, and creased her face into what she probably thought was a reassuring smile.

Petty Potts's reassuring smiles never really worked somehow. Danny grabbed on to a little leather strap above the window and narrowed his eyes at her.

Josh did the same.

'Oh, for heaven's sake, you two!' she huffed, as she turned back and started to drive up the road in a lurching fashion. 'You might have a little faith in me. I'm not going to kill you!'

Danny and Josh raised identical eyebrows at her in the rear-view mirror. Petty had never *tried* to kill them, true. But she had certainly brought them closer to a bizarre and grisly death than any other grown-up they knew. Since they'd stumbled into the secret underground laboratory hidden beneath her garden shed, they'd very nearly been crushed, drowned, splatted, pecked hollow, swatted, mummified and eaten—more times than they wanted to remember. Petty might *look* like a nice old biddy, but she was the genius inventor of SWITCH spray, which could change you into a creepy-crawly with just a few squirts. Josh and Danny had already been transformed into spiders and flies—and that was really quite enough.

Naming her *Serum Which Instigates Total Cellular Hijack* 'SWITCH' made it sound rather fun. And it was—if you didn't mind getting eaten, drowned, turned into soup or splattered with a giant sandal.

'Any more side effects from your house fly adventure?' Petty called back, cheerfully, over the rumble and clunk of the fifty-year-old engine.

'No. We've stopped sniffing around the bin now,' said Josh. 'And Danny hasn't spat on a doughnut or tried to walk up the kitchen window since last Tuesday.' He sighed and then grinned to himself. Being a bluebottle *was* very exciting. Even Danny had loved it—well, apart from the bit when he'd been on the lunch menu for a hungry spider.

'Good, good, good,' said Petty. 'You know, I thought it was a disaster when you two first accidentally ran into a jet of my Spider SWITCH spray . . . but actually it was the best thing that could have happened. If you hadn't found your way into my secret lab, I might never have moved on from trying to SWITCH rats and dogs!'

'Er . . . thanks,' muttered Josh, raising his eyebrows at Danny, who was shaking his head and looking annoyed. The dog Petty had been trying to spray was *their* dog, Piddle. It was when they were rescuing Piddle that they had first got caught in a jet of Petty's SWITCH spray.

'And, of course, rats could never tell me what the experience was like!' went on Petty. 'And you two are *so* helpful! I'm so delighted you've agreed to be my assistants on the S.W.I.T.C.H. project.'

'Look—we just said we'd help you out by looking for your missing cube things,' said Josh as they reached the traffic lights near their school. 'We're *not* trying out any more SWITCH sprays!'

'I never asked you to!' protested Petty, looking all innocent and injured. 'And finding my missing cubes is absolutely the most important thing. Without them I will never be able to rediscover my formula and move on to turning things into reptiles—and you'll never get the chance to find out how it feels to be a giant python or an anaconda or a Komodo dragon!'

'We don't *want* to find out!' squawked Danny. 'Haven't you heard us? Being turned into other creatures is just too dangerous!'

'Yes, of course, of course . . . ' Petty smiled ferociously into her rear-view mirror. 'Although I

can't imagine how anyone could hurt you if you were a twenty-four foot python!'

Danny and Josh looked at each other—and there was just the faintest twinkle of excitement in Josh's eyes. He thought about Petty's promise. If they could find the last four missing cubes which held the secret of the REPTOSWITCH spray, she would be able to temporarily turn them into amazing reptiles. Josh loved wildlife—being a lizard or a snake would be incredible! The BUGSWITCH was amazing enough but a REPTOSWITCH? It would be hard to resist trying *that* spray out. And nice to be less easy to eat or squash! This was a definite downside to being a creepy-crawly.

'Josh!' hissed Danny, narrowing his eyes at his brother. 'Don't even *think* about it! You don't even know she's telling the truth! She's as fishy as fishfingers in fish sauce in a fish-shaped dish!'

Josh had to admit Danny was right. Petty claimed some pretty mad things. Although she had the BUGSWITCH sprays sorted, she insisted a man who had worked with her had stolen the rest of her research and even burnt out bits of her memory. She'd forgotten where she'd hidden the special glass cubes which contained the secret REPTOSWITCH formula. That was why she needed their help—to find them. And they *had* found one.

'We have been looking for your cubes,' Danny was saying. 'And we will keep looking for them. But don't go thinking you'll *ever* change us into anything again—not unless we agree to it!'

'Well, of course not! What do you take me for? Some kind of monster?' huffed Petty. 'I would never dream of such a thing. But . . . I just wanted to tell you that I think I have perfected a SWITCH *potion* now. You can *drink* SWITCH instead of spray it on—and it'll have the same effect.'

'We're not drinking *anything*!' declared Josh.

'Of course you're not—but if you ever *did*, it's all quite safe because, look, there's a SWITCH antidote potion too! I made it just in case drinking SWITCH makes the changes last longer than the spray. It gets right inside, of course, so it probably lasts longer—but the antidote can stop it all at any time like the gas back in my lab. Look—I've got both the potion and the antidote in my bag.'

With one hand on the wheel, she turned
around to rummage in the bag between them and
was just hauling out a small plastic bottle when
Josh shouted,

'LOOK OUT!'

There was a screech of elderly brakes and all three of them jerked violently forward as Petty's Morris Traveller nearly collided with the lollipop man. School bags, lunchboxes, and Petty's stuff went flying everywhere and it was just as well Josh and Danny had been hanging on to the little leather straps above their heads or they might well have shot through the windscreen.

Petty had bashed her nose on her steering wheel. 'Oh, all right! All right! Keep your stupid shiny hat on!' she was shouting at the lollipop man who was waving his yellow STOP sign around and looking very angry.

'Please—just drive around the corner, so we can get out,' wailed Josh keeping his head down behind the front seats in case anyone from their school was watching. He and Danny scrabbled about, picking up their bags and books and lunchboxes.

'My bun's all squashed!' moaned Danny, picking up a cake which now looked more like a biscuit.

'Well, mine had a pretty hard whack too, thanks for your concern!' sniffed Petty, as they pulled at last around the corner, away from the angry lollipop man.

'My buNNN! BuNNN—not BUM!' squawked Danny, with a horrified shudder.

'Thanks for the lift,' said Josh as they fumbled with the tipping front seat and the passenger door. He and Danny grabbed their school stuff and got out as fast as they could, slamming the door behind them.

Petty rubbed her nose, and called out, 'I'm off round the park to try the potion and the antidote out on the squirrels. I'll let you know how it goes!' and she did a violent U-turn, nearly knocking a passing postman off his bike.

'Come on,' said Danny, shoving his bottle of drink and flattened bun back into his lunchbox and slinging his bag over his shoulder. 'I never thought I'd say this, but I can't wait to get to school, where it's safe.'

And he went on through the school gates, having no idea that something very, very *un*safe was slurping about in his bag.

FUN AND GAMES

There are more games for you to play and download free on the S.W.I.T.C.H. website.

www.switch-books.co.uk

Word search

Search for the hidden words listed below:

TOPIARY	JOSH
TARQUIN	DANNY
SHARPE	PETTY POTTS
FLY	RAT
GARDEN	CAKE
ROCKERY	SPIDER
DRAGON	SWITCH

T	A	P	S	N	O	G	A	R	D
O	C	A	K	E	B	W	N	U	V
P	E	T	T	Y	P	O	T	T	S
I	N	F	L	L	T	H	P	A	W
A	D	J	I	F	R	Q	F	R	I
R	O	C	K	E	R	Y	A	Q	T
Y	L	F	D	A	N	N	Y	U	C
T	W	I	O	R	T	R	O	I	H
M	P	C	G	A	R	D	E	N	E
S	H	A	R	P	E	H	S	O	J

Answers on page 122

Spot the difference

These pictures *look* the same, but can you spot ten differences?

Answers on page 122

Are you a bug boffin?

Question 1)
WHAT FOOD AND DRINK DOES PETTY
POTTS PREPARE FOR THE BOYS WHEN
THEY GO TO HER HOUSE?
A) Iced sponge cake and orange
squash
B) Fly sandwiches and chocolate
milkshakes
C) Hamburgers and coke

Question 2)
WHO IS VICTOR CROUCH?
A) The judge for the Best Garden
competition
B) The spider who tries to eat
Danny
C) Petty Potts's arch enemy

Question 3)
HOW DOES JOSH ESCAPE MRS
SHARPE'S HOUSE?
A) Through the front door
B) Through the front room window
C) Through the kitchen door

Question 4)
WHAT KIND OF INSECT DO JOSH AND
DANNY TURN INTO?
A) Bluebottle flies
B) Spiders
C) Cluster flies

Question 5)
WHAT IS MRS SHARPE'S SON
CALLED?
A) Darwin
B) Archibald
C) Tarquin

Question 6)
WHAT DOES JOSH DO TO DISTRACT
MRS SHARPE?
A) He makes a loud noise
B) He tickles her toes
C) He flies up her nostril

Question 7)
WHO EATS A SPIDER IN THE STORY?
A) Scratch
B) Danny
C) Mrs Sharpe

Question 8)
WHERE DO SCRATCH AND SNIFF LIVE?
A) In Mrs Sharpe's living room
B) Under the shed in Josh and
Danny's garden
C) In Petty Potts's laboratory

Answers on page 123

Missing pieces

Can you work out which piece of the puzzle is missing?

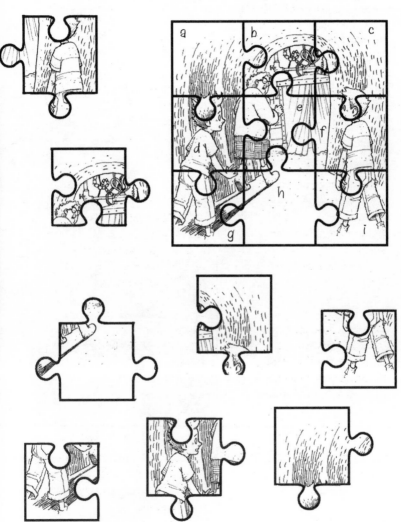

Answers

Word Search (page 118)

T	A	P	S	N	O	G	A	R	D
O	C	A	K	E	B	W	N	U	V
P	E	T	T	Y	P	O	T	T	S
I	N	F	L	L	T	H	P	A	W
A	D	J	I	F	R	Q	F	R	I
R	O	C	K	E	R	Y	A	Q	T
Y	L	F	D	A	N	N	Y	U	C
T	W	I	O	R	T	R	O	I	H
M	P	C	G	A	R	D	E	N	E
S	H	A	R	P	E	H	S	O	J

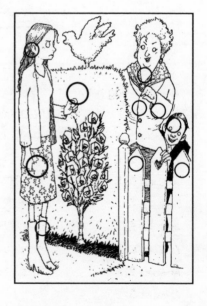

Spot the difference
(page 119)

122

Answers

Missing pieces
(page 121)

Are you a bug boffin?
(page 120)

Answer 1) A

Answer 2) C

Answer 3) B

Answer 4) A

Answer 5) C

Answer 6) C

Answer 7) A

Answer 8) B

Give yourself a point for every question you got right.

6–8 POINTS — You are a real bug boffin! Nothing gets past you.

3–5 POINTS — You are SWITCHed on! You enjoy a good adventure.

0–2 POINTS — Oh dear, looks as if you need to brush up on your bug skills! Better luck next time!

About the author

Ali Sparkes grew up in the woods of Hampshire. Actually, strictly speaking she grew up in a house in Hampshire. The woods were great but lacked basic facilities like sofas and a well stocked fridge. Nevertheless, the woods were where she and her friends spent much of their time and so Ali grew up with a deep and abiding love of wildlife. If you ever see Ali with a large garden spider on her shoulder she will most likely be screeching 'AAAAAAAAAARRRRRGHGETITOFFME!'

Ali lives in Southampton with her husband and sons and would never kill a creepy-crawly of any kind. They are more scared of her than she is of them. (Creepy-crawlies, not her husband and sons.)

Other books
in the  series

Spider Stampede

Grasshopper Glitch

Ant Attack

Crane Fly Crash

Beetle Blast

S.W.I.T.C.H.
SERUM WHICH INSTIGATES TOTAL CELLULAR HIJACK

Whether you're interested in insects
or terrified of tarantulas, you'll love the
S.W.I.T.C.H. website!

Find out more about the bugs in
Josh and Danny's adventures, enter fantastic
competitions, read the first chapters
of all of the S.W.I.T.C.H. books, and enjoy
creepy-crawly games and activities.

www.switch-books.co.uk